Belvedere

RIVER TOWN

BONNIE and ARTHUR GEISERT

HOUGHTON MIFFLIN COMPANY BOSTON 1999

Walter Lorraine Books

for Steve

Walter Lorraine *wl* Books

Text Copyright © 1999 by Bonnie Geisert
Illustrations Copyright © 1999 by Arthur Geisert

Library of Congress Cataloging-in-Publication Data
Geisert, Bonnie.
    River town / Bonnie and Arthur Geisert.
        p.   cm.
    Summary: Describes, in brief text and illustrations, a year in the
life of a river bank town and the many changes that occur throughout
the seasons.
    ISBN 0-395-90891-4
    1. Cities and towns—United States—Juvenile literature.
2. Harbors—United States—Juvenile literature.   3. River life—
United States—Juvenile literature.   4. Seasons—United States—
Juvenile literature.   [1. Cities and towns.   2. Rivers.
3. Seasons.]   I. Geisert, Arthur.   II. Title..
HT123.G423   1999   98-17249
307.72'0973—dc21   CIP
                                                    AC
Printed in the United States of America
HOR 10 9 8 7 6 5 4 3 2 1

On the banks of America's rivers there are many towns. During the eighteenth and nineteenth centuries, the towns grew where fur trappers set up trading posts, where ferries crossed the rivers, where mines yielded rich ores, and where supply points for boats and trains were needed.

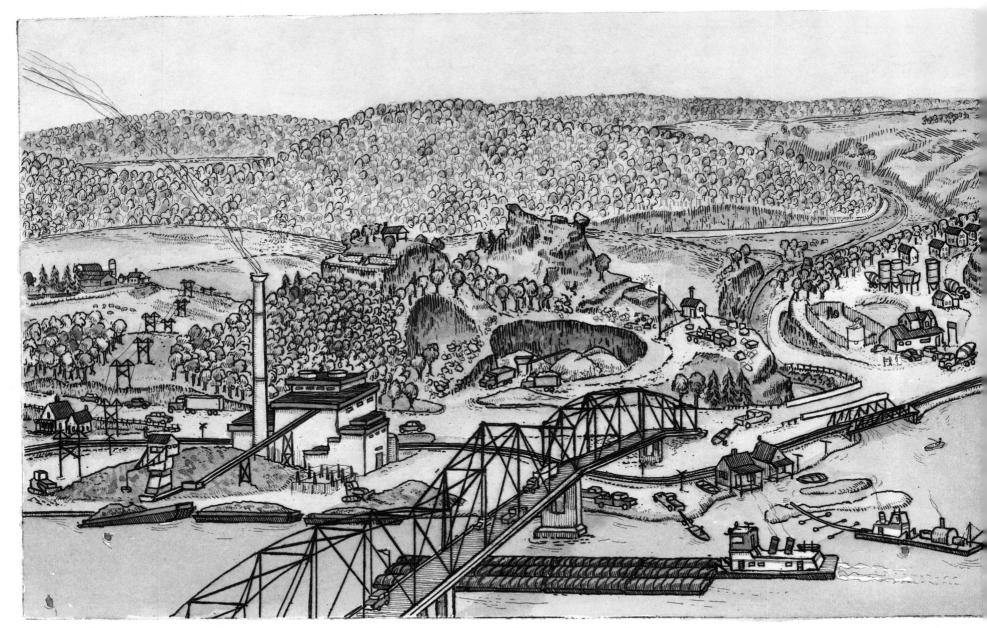

The river town is busy in the fall. Towboats move barges loaded
with coal and grain up and down the river.

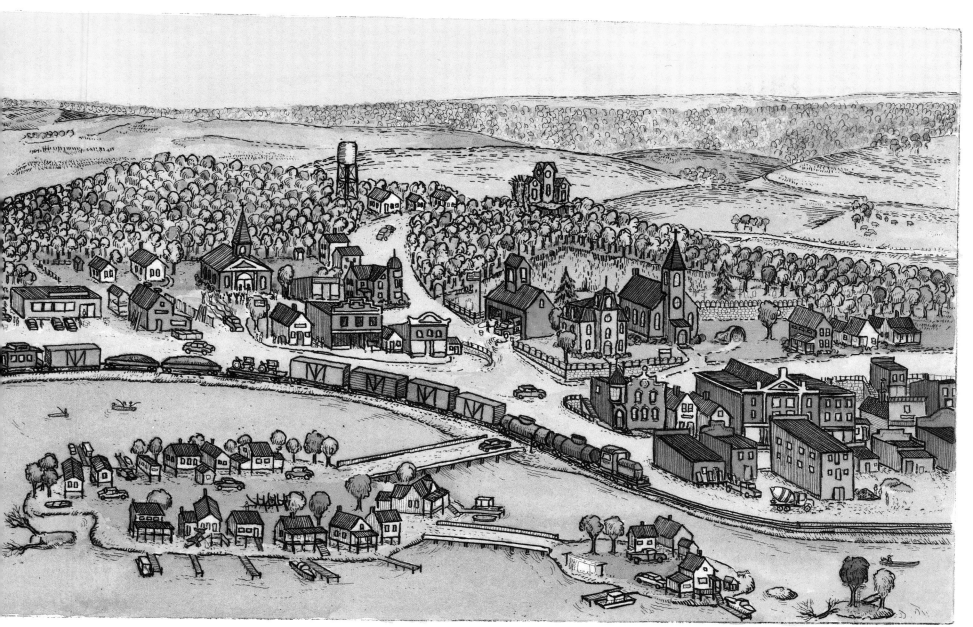

Trains carry cargo along its edge and inland for later sale and shipment
to countries around the world.

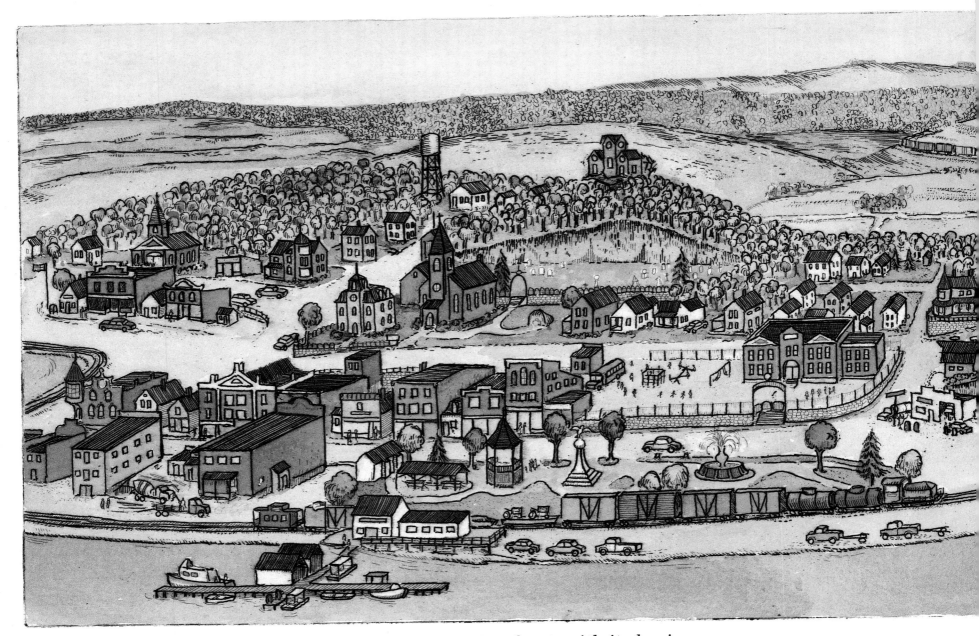

The town is often built in levels. First is the riverfront, with its businesses in sturdy buildings where goods are stored and sold.

Set back are the churches and houses, often with lookout towers.
Beyond are farms that rely on the river for moving their produce.

When the fall harvest is under way, trucks are filled with grain
and driven to the terminal in the town.

After the trucks unload their tons of grain at the terminal, the grain is loaded onto barges and trains to be shipped to all parts of the world.

Halloween foretells the end of fall and the beginning of winter.
It is a time to turn from work to play.

Everyone joins in the fun. Residents line up along Main Street
to see the floats and the people in costumes marching by.

In winter, the loud blast of a towboat's horn is not heard. The river
is frozen over, and the towboat companies have taken their barges south.

River business is slow, but the trains still run. They blow their whistles at the crossings while people go about their winter work.

Now people stay inside their warm buildings and look out
on their town and on the river.

Occasionally a migrating eagle can be seen swooping down to a patch of open water near a dam to catch a fish.

The river becomes a playground of ice for the children.
Ice fishing is a way to get fresh food.

In winter, the café is always a good place to go. People gather for food and warmth, to debate world events, and to exchange the latest town news.

As the warm days of spring thaw the ice and the snow on the hills melts,
the river begins to rise.

With rain it continues to rise until water covers the small islands.
People have to use boats instead of cars to get to shore.

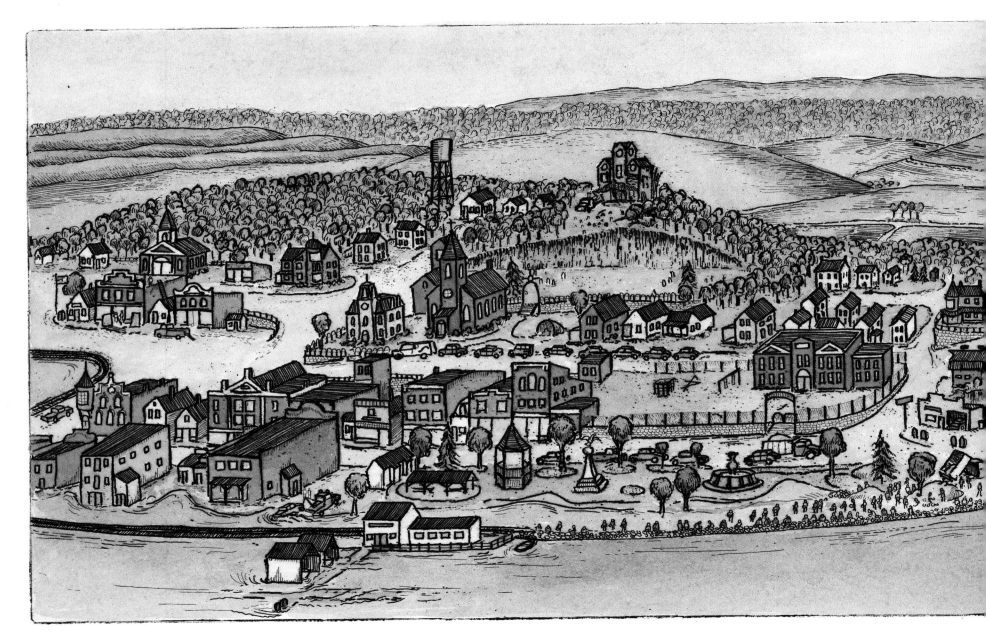

Day by day the people watch the river with concern.
Too much water can bring the threat of floods.

The people build a levee of sandbags to hold back the water and protect the town.

The rain stops. The levee holds and the river settles back into its banks.
The land dries and the farmers prepare their fields for spring planting.

In the schoolyard, children delight in playing in the sun. The towboats
and their barges are welcomed on the riverfront.

The townspeople gather to enjoy the warming weather.

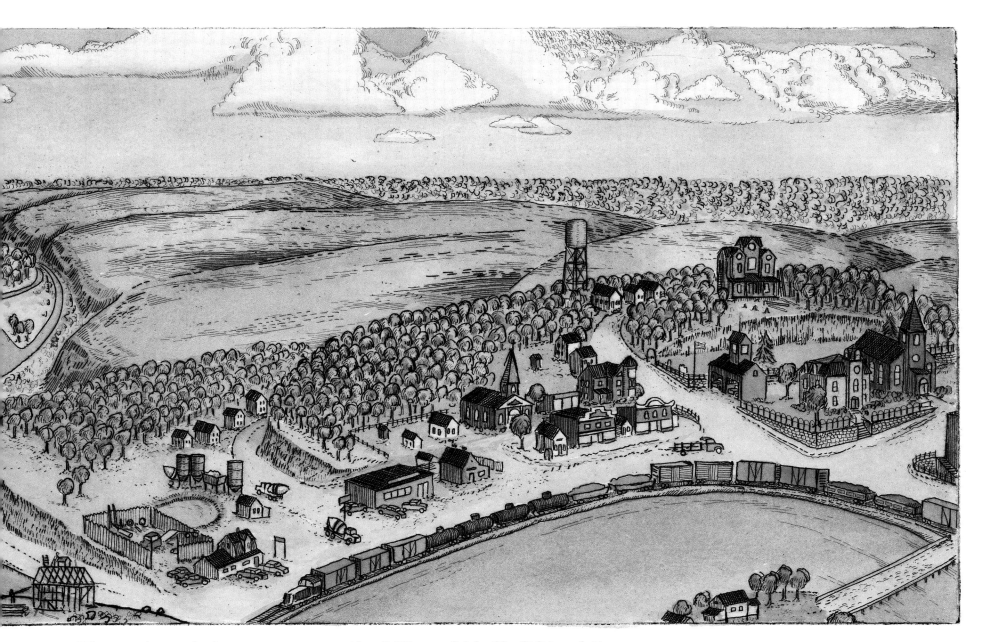

The spring wind sweeps across the hills and bluffs, lifting kites
and chasing fog from the river and the hollows.

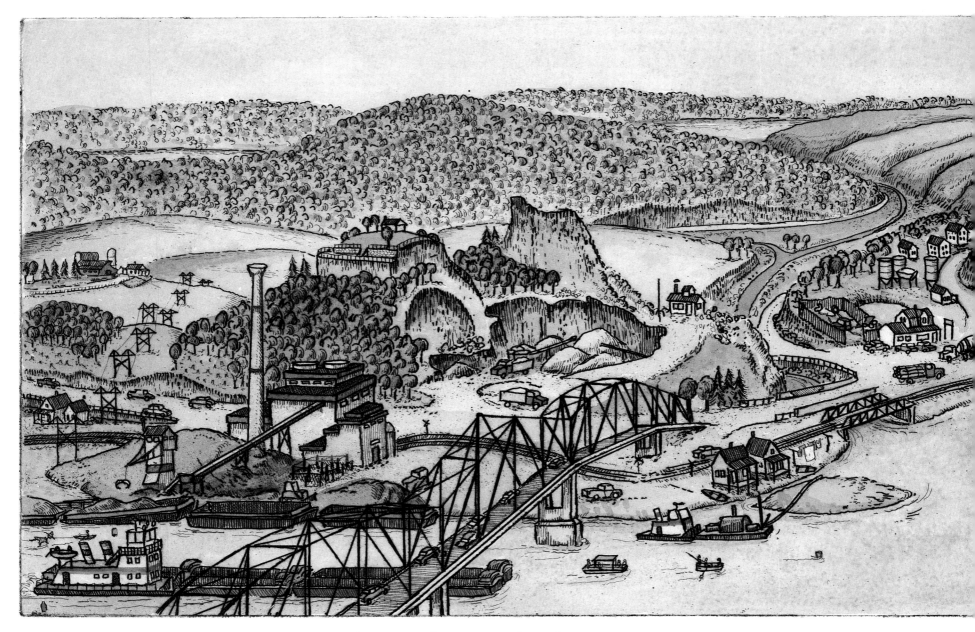

It is summer. The river is again busy with tows and trains.

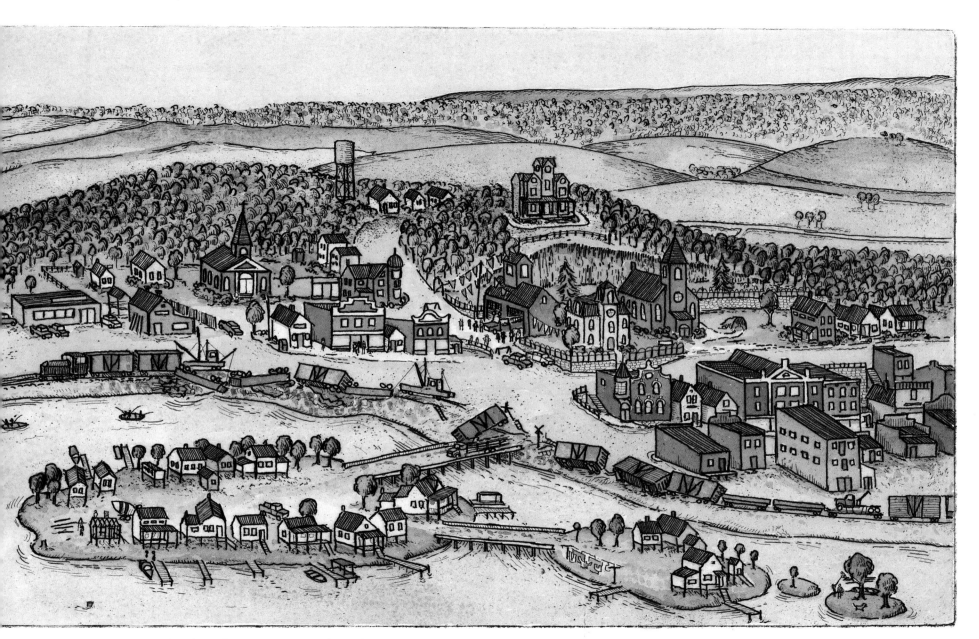

Buoys mark the deep channels where captains guide the barges.

Train engineers must go slowly on the town's curving tracks.

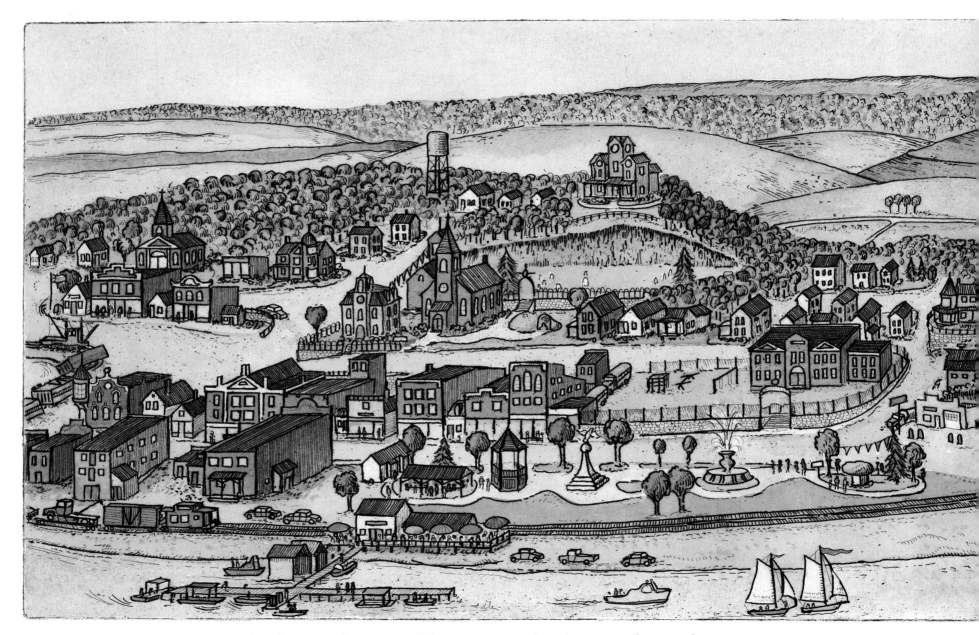

Summer is a time for fun on the river. There are gatherings at the park.
There are boating parties and dock parties.

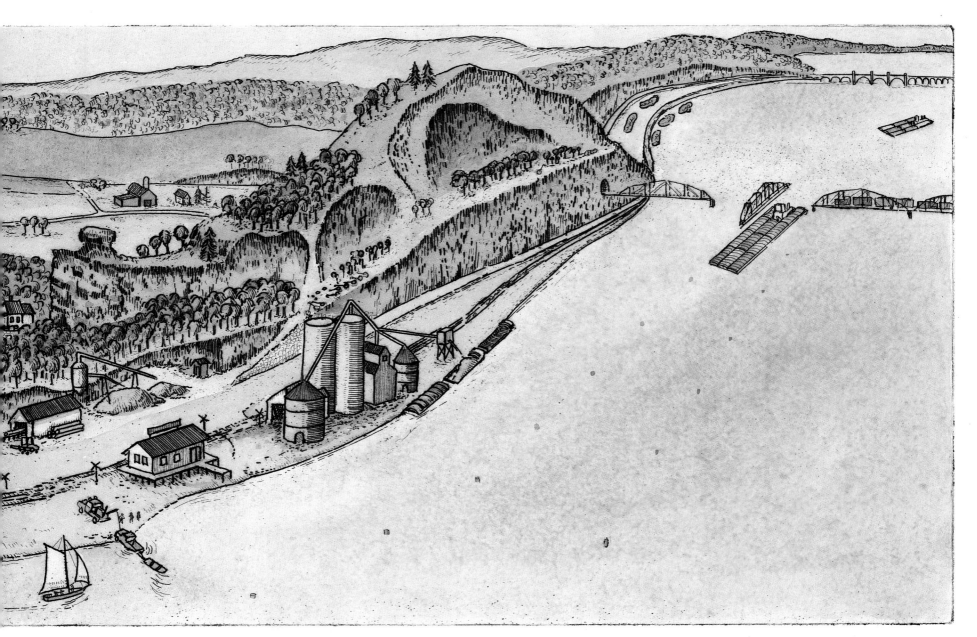

Sailboats, houseboats, pleasure boats, and fishing boats all share
the river with the towboats and barges.

There is time to build a tree house on an island.

And there is time to watch the river.

A year has passed in the river town. It was a year of challenge and change caused by nature and by man. Stories of the people's daily life and how they faced the challenges can be seen in the illustrations.

The river, an obvious challenge during the spring flood, took a Halloween witch for an uncharted ride and displaced an island dog to a rooftop lookout. At times, vehicles ended up in the river and needed towing help to get out.

No one was hurt when a large boulder rolled down the side of the quarry and crushed the office, boom truck, and bridge. The smashed truck was hauled to the junkyard. Luckily, the new boom truck escaped damage in the train wreck. The boulder was given a special place in the park.

Some places in town have changed their shape. A huge coal pile was consumed and then replenished. The stone and gravel quarry widened as its rock was removed for construction material. The dredging machine removed silt from river channels and new islands were formed.

Rock, lumber from the sawmill, and concrete from the cement plant were used to build roads, rock walls, an addition to a warehouse by the river, a new barn to replace the one that burned down, a new house and boat on the island, and a new quarry office. A bridge was repaired and a mansion on the hill was restored. A Main Street building was fixed up and a new business opened there.

There were celebrations in the town. The firefighters held an open house. A wedding took place. A funeral was observed. And in a summer ceremony, the boulder was dedicated as a monument to remind people of earth's natural resources and their many uses.